Party in the castle

Collect all the

LITTLE SPARKLES

1. Party in the Garden
2. Party at the Zoo
3. Party at the Pool
4. Party on the Pirate Ship
5. Party in the Castle

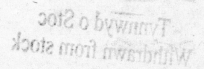

Little Sparkles

Party in the Castle

Emily Moon

Illustrated by Aaron Zenz

SCHOLASTIC

First published in the UK in 2012 by Scholastic Children's Books
An imprint of Scholastic Ltd
Euston House, 24 Eversholt Street
London, NW1 1DB, UK
Registered office: Westfield Road, Southam, Warwickshire, CV47 0RA
SCHOLASTIC and associated logos are trademarks and/or
registered trademarks of Scholastic Inc.
Series created by Working Partners Ltd.

Text copyright © Working Partners Ltd., 2012
Illustration copyright © Aaron Zenz, 2012

ISBN 978 1407 12460 5

A CIP catalogue record for this book
is available from the British Library.

Printed and bound by CPI Group (UK) Ltd., Croydon, CR0 4YY
Papers used by Scholastic Children's Books
are made from wood grown in sustainable forests.

13 5 7 9 10 8 6 4 2

This is a work of fiction. Names, characters, places,
incidents and dialogues are products of the author's imagination
or are used fictitiously. Any resemblance to actual people, living
or dead, events or locales is entirely coincidental.

www.scholastic.co.uk/zone

With special thanks to Jane Clarke

To Catherine and Adelaide

Party Time!
It's our birthday
on Sunday.
Please come
and celebrate
at Fitzroy Castle
at eleven a.m.
There will be games
and a birthday banquet
It's fancy dress,
so dress fancy!

Lots of love,
Holly and Rose

1

Let the Party Begin!

"Welcome to your very own Birthday Banquet, Princess Holly and Princess Rose!" Mum announced.

Holly and Rose jumped up and down, gleefully clapping their hands. They were in a meadow beside Fitzroy Castle. A moat filled with water flowed around the castle's grounds, and the castle's flags fluttered in the gentle breeze. There was another kind of castle across the grass,

too – a bouncy castle. It was so exciting!

Mum swept off a plastic covering to reveal a feast laid out on a silvery tablecloth. There were platters piled high with fruit kebabs, chicken drumsticks and crown-shaped sandwiches, and pitchers of pink lemonade with gold plastic goblets to drink from.

In the middle was a beautiful, white-iced birthday cake in the shape of a castle. It had turrets made from upside-down ice cream cones and was decorated with tiny pink and green icing flowers, with silver sugar-ball centres.

"Wow! Our favourite colours!" Rose exclaimed in delight. She looked like a fairy-tale princess in her long, flowing pink dress with floaty sleeves. It perfectly matched her pink watch.

"The turrets are the same shape as our hats," Holly giggled, spinning round to make her soft green dress, and the scarf on top of her pointy hat, swirl. She checked her green watch. "The guests will be here any minute," she whispered excitedly to her twin sister. "I really, really hope the Little Sparkles turn up, too."

"I can't wait to see them again!" Rose agreed, thinking of the magical little puppy, pony, kitten, bunny and turtle who were their secret friends. "But the last Party Pooper better stay away. It would be awful if he came to our party too."

The twins shared a worried glance. The five Poopers were naughty creatures who tried to ruin parties. They'd caused lots of trouble, but Holly and Rose had been able to help the Little Sparkles get rid of them. Now, there was only one Pooper left. But one Pooper could do a

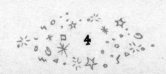

lot of damage!

"Here are your guests!" Dad's voice broke into the twins' thoughts. Their friends were laughing excitedly as they raced across the drawbridge that lay over the moat. Everyone had dressed up. Jenny was with a bunch of princesses wearing pretty dresses and tiaras, and Hari led a small group of knights in shiny plastic armour.

"Maisie's a jester!" laughed Holly, pointing out a girl wearing a costume decorated with red and yellow diamonds and a floppy three-pointed hat. Walking beside her was what looked like a small green dinosaur with wings.

"Billy's come as a dragon!" Rose giggled.

The twins welcomed their friends and thanked them for the carefully wrapped presents they had brought. Mum put them in two piles, one for each twin.

"For later," she said.

"When can we have a go on the bouncy castle?" Billy asked.

"There's no hurry, I've booked it for the day," Dad said with a smile.

"We'll go on it after the party games," Rose added. "We can play Hide-and-Seek and Musical Tiaras. . ."

". . .and Silver Slipper Race and Pin the Tail on the Knight's Steed!" Holly declared excitedly. "What shall we start with?"

"Pin the Tail!" Maisie jangled the bells on her jester's stick.

Everyone gathered around a big picture Dad had drawn of a tail-less horse, set up on an old school board. Rose took a silver sash and bound it round Maisie's eyes. Holly put a fake tail

made from straw in Maisie's free hand. Then the twins put their hands on Maisie's shoulders and gently turned her around and around, making the jester bells jingle.

"I feel dizzy!" Maisie squealed, lurching forward. She jabbed at the air a couple of times, missed the picture board entirely – and stuck the tail on a plate of sandwiches! She pushed up the blindfold.

"Yummy! Tail sandwich!" she exclaimed.

Everyone laughed.

"Our party's started really well," Holly whispered to Rose. "Maybe the Pooper won't come after all…"

POP!

There was a noise like a thousand balloons bursting at once.

It was the bouncy castle!

"It's exploded!" Billy shrieked, racing towards it. Mum, Dad and the other party guests hurried after him.

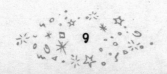

The twins looked at each other.

"It must be the Party Pooper!" Rose groaned. "He'll spoil everything unless the Little Sparkles help us stop him!"

"But what if they don't come?" Holly murmured. "Without them, our party will be ruined!"

2

Looking for Trouble

Suddenly, the air filled with a sweet tinkling sound like fairy bells. Holly and Rose glanced up as five tiny shimmering clouds drifted down, sprinkling them with brightly coloured glitter.

But the twins knew that they weren't clouds – they were magical little creatures, each carrying a tiny party bag!

"You came!" the twins squealed in delight as Bubbles the pink bunny, Peppy the blue puppy and Tikki the yellow kitten landed on Rose's shoulders. Princess the purple and white pony galloped with glee round Holly's pointy hat, making a sparkling purple and white ring, while Tubbs the rainbow turtle chased after her. In their tinkling voices, the Little Sparkles sang:

"Happy Birthday, Rose and Holly
May your day be bright and jolly!"

Tubbs spun on the point of Holly's hat, his shell flashing all the colours of the rainbow.

"We're very sorry the Pooper got here first," he said.

"Don't worry," said Rose, reaching up to pat Tubbs's tiny head. "Now you're here, we can stop him. We're a team, remember?"

"We just need to catch that mean old Pooper and make him enjoy himself!" Holly agreed.

The Little Sparkles nodded their heads. Together, they'd already turned four Poopers into Little Sparkles by persuading them to have fun.

"It'll be hard to find the Pooper and keep everything secret from our friends," Rose pointed out. Holly and Rose were the only people who could see or hear the Poopers and Little Sparkles. Even if they shared their wonderful secret, the twins didn't think anyone would believe them.

The party guests returned from the bouncy castle, looking glum. Nearly all the air had escaped now. The castle's turrets and walls were flopping over and the section for jumping up and down was as flat as the ground.

"We'll have to do something else," Billy sighed.

Holly looked meaningfully at Rose, and then turned to their friends.

"I know!" she said. "Let's play hide-and-seek. We'll be the seekers."

"That's cheating; there are two of you!" Billy declared.

"We promise to stick together," Rose reassured him.

"Like we always do," Holly added.

"We can look for the Pooper while we

play!" Holly whispered to Rose and the Little Sparkles. The tiny creatures zipped off as the twins covered their eyes with their hands and began to count. . .

Everyone, including Mum and Dad, dashed off to hide.

"...Ninety-eight, ninety-nine, one hundred!" the twins cried together. "Ready or not, here we come!"

Holly and Rose rushed towards the Little Sparkles. They were hovering near a rustling bush, chiming excitedly.

"It must be the Pooper!" Rose hissed as they crept towards the greenery. She peered beneath it, hoping to see the flubby, grubby little creature. But instead there was a flash of yellow and red and a jangling of bells.

"Maisie!" the twins breathed, as their friend crawled out with her jester

costume covered in leaves. "Found you!"

Peppy gave an excited little yap. Something was shuffling behind a nearby tree.

"That sounds like the Pooper," Holly hissed. "Quick! Grab him!" She and Rose rounded the huge old oak tree and pounced.

"You got me!" Dad laughed.

There was a sneeze from a patch of long dry grass and Mum's head popped up.

"Sorry, it's too itchy to stay still!" Mum explained.

"We're finding everyone too quickly," Rose whispered. "We need to make this game last until we find the Pooper. Don't pounce unless you're sure it's him!"

But every time they were certain that they'd discovered the Pooper's hiding place, it turned out to be one of the party guests. On the other side of the meadow, Princess found a green hummock of grass that was really only Billy in his dragon costume. And the rumbly grumbly noise

Tubbs heard in the hedge was Jenny's
hungry tummy.

Soon, Holly, Rose and the Little
Sparkles had searched the whole
meadow and found all the guests, but
they still couldn't find the Pooper!

"We need a new plan," Holly
murmured.

The Little Sparkles jingled their agreement.

"What should we do now?" asked Rose.

But before anyone could answer, there was a loud, soggy, squelchy noise. THHHP! A tennis-ball-sized creature that looked like a bad-tempered lump of mud landed right next to the twins' feet.

"We can stop searching now," Holly declared. "The Pooper has found us!"

3

King of the castle

The Little Sparkles jangled in alarm as the blobby creature screwed up his face and waved his stumpy little arms. He yelled:

"I'm a Party Pooper, I poop everything.
I'm the final Pooper. I'm the Pooper king!"

Then he blew a loud raspberry at Holly, Rose and the Little Sparkles and blobbed off towards the gateway that led into Fitzroy Castle.

"He'll spoil the visitors' day out!" Rose gasped, but her words were drowned by a loud wail.

"Holly, Rose, come quick!" Billy yelled. He was standing by the party games. The Little Sparkles whizzed towards him in a flash of rainbow glitter.

The twins raced after them and skidded to a halt. The tiaras were shattered into tiny pieces, the heels had been broken off the silver slippers, and Dad's drawing of the horse was in tatters.

"He's destroyed our party!" Holly groaned.

There was worse to come. The banqueting table was covered in muddy footprints, and so was their lovely birthday cake. The ice-cream cone turrets were in bits, the beautiful icing flowers were smashed, and every one of the sandwiches had bite marks in them.

"The feast!" Rose cried.

Mum, Dad and the party guests were staring open-mouthed at the mess.

Unheard by anyone else, Tikki sang sweetly in the twins' ears:

"Princess friends, please don't feel blue,
The Little Sparkles will help you!"

Holly and Rose breathed a secret sigh of relief, but everyone else was still upset.

"Whoever has done this is very mean," Dad said seriously. "But we can't let it ruin the party."

Mum tried to smile as she opened a leaflet about Fitzroy Castle.

"There are lots of activities going on at the castle today," she said, showing it to Holly and Rose. "Everyone can join in."

Rose pointed to a picture of an archery target.

"I'd like to try that," she declared.

"Me too!" Billy stated.

"I'd like to make a shield," Holly announced.

Rose looked surprised. They usually chose to do the same things.

"If we divide up, we'll have more chance of finding the Pooper," Holly explained in a quiet voice.

"Oh, yes!" Rose whispered back. "We can take it in turns to slip away and

27

search the castle with the Little Sparkles."

Holly looked at her green watch. "We'll change over at twelve o'clock," she agreed.

Everyone headed towards Fitzroy Castle, past the giant wooden catapult that had once been used to attack it. Rose waved goodbye to Holly, Dad and half of the party guests, including Hari and Maisie, as they hurried through the ancient stone gateway into the inner courtyard. Then Rose, Mum and the other guests walked over to a row of targets set up outside the castle walls. The Little Sparkles flew close to Rose, twinkling in the sunshine.

Rose watched the archery instructor standing near the targets. He was dressed like Robin Hood and he handed out plastic bows and arrows with suckers on the tips.

"Princesses always go first!" he said, sweeping off his feather-tipped hat. He showed Rose how to fit the notch at the end of the arrow on to the bowstring.

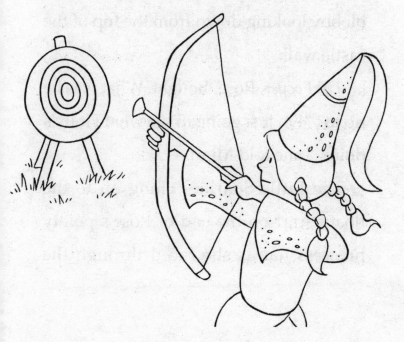

Rose pulled the bowstring back and pointed the arrow upwards, before sweeping it down towards the target and letting the arrow fly. Her shot just missed the bullseye.

Rose turned to hand the bow to Billy. But from the corner of her eye, she spotted something mud-coloured and blobby looking down from the top of the castle wall.

The Pooper, Rose thought. What was he up to? "I'm just going to see what Holly's doing," she told Mum.

The Little Sparkles clung on to the floaty scarf on the end of Rose's pointy princess hat as she raced through the

gateway. She turned sharply at the base of one of the turrets, and stuck her head into the dark spiral staircase that led to the battlement wall around the castle. She could hear chanting echoing down the old stone steps.

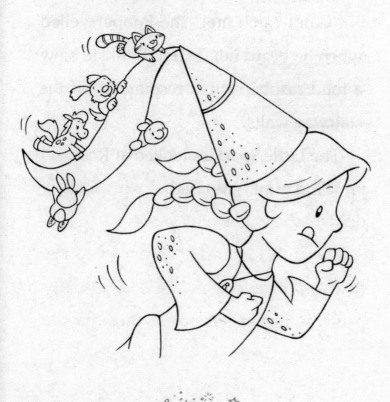

"I'm a naughty rascal!
I'm the king of the castle!"

Rose instantly knew who it was. "The Pooper's here!" she exclaimed. "But where's he hiding?"

"Can't catch me!" the Pooper yelled when he heard her. THHHPPP! He blew a loud raspberry that resounded off the stairway walls.

The Little Sparkles looked at Rose.

"Find him!" she cried.

4

Flying High

There was a swirl of twinkling light as the Little Sparkles zippety-zapped up the dark spiral staircase. Rose raced up the steps so fast that her head began to spin and she had to put out her hands to steady herself against the cold stone walls. As she stepped out on to the narrow walkway that ran around the top of the castle, she tripped over Tubbs. He was on his back, whirling round on his rainbow shell.

"I'm spinning the other way to stop feeling dizzy! Those stairs made me feel funny," he explained.

When Tubbs stopped spinning, Rose gently turned him back over on to his front. Then she held on to the safety rail and looked over a low section of the wall. She could see across the meadow and the moat to the rolling hills in the distance.

"Wow!" she breathed, turning to look inside the castle. It was built like a hollow square with turrets on the corners and a courtyard in the middle. Hanging down from the battlements were huge banners made of cloth. Each was decorated with a different creature. Rose could see a lion, a dragon and a unicorn. *It's as if the castle's got its own Little Sparkles to look after it*, she thought.

The courtyard was packed with stalls selling refreshments and souvenirs, and tables were set up for different crafts. She could see Holly and her group sitting at one of the tables, making shields.

"Look, there's Holly!" said Rose, pointing to them. But the Little Sparkles were staring in a different direction.

"Neigh!" Princess whinnied excitedly and began to prance, sprinkling Rose with glitter from her tail. The other Little Sparkles twinkled and jingled urgently as they pointed along the parapet. Rose followed their gaze. They'd found the Party Pooper! The flubby, blubby creature was bothering a group of tourists. One of the tourists had a camera and he leapt up on the man's shoulders and pulled his hair to make him jump.

"He's pooping their pictures! Stop him!" Rose hurtled towards the visitors while the Little Sparkles soared over her head like magical sparkly thistledown. When the tourists saw Rose rushing towards them, they flattened themselves against the wall.

"She's in a hurry," said the man with the camera.

THHHPPP! The Pooper leapt on to the battlements and launched himself towards the banner decorated with a unicorn.

"Bye byeee!" he yelled as he slid down it, towards the courtyard below.

There was a rainbow flash of light as the Little Sparkles swooped after him. Rose raced down the nearest spiral staircase into the busy courtyard. It was full of stalls and people enjoying their day out, but there was no sign of the Pooper.

Peppy sniffed at the banner, trying to pick up a scent.

His ears drooped. "He didn't leave a

trail," he sighed.

"That horrid old Pooper got away again!" Rose groaned. She glanced at her pink watch. It was twelve o'clock, and time to get back to her group. She'd done her best. Would Holly be able to do any better?

5

Ice Cream Surprise

Holly was gluing one last animal shape on to her cardboard shield as Rose raced up.

"You put the Little Sparkles on your shield!" Rose exclaimed. Holly was proud of the colourful puppy, kitten, bunny, pony and turtle that she'd decorated the front with.

"Princess Rose!" Dad sounded surprised. "I thought you were doing archery."

"Rose has come to show me something," Holly explained, linking hands with her twin. "We'll be back soon!"

Rose pulled Holly towards the unicorn banner. The Little Sparkles floated beside it, waving excitedly.

"We saw the Pooper slide down here," Rose told her.

"That means he must be in the courtyard somewhere," said Holly.

Rose nodded. "Good luck!" she said.

"I've got to get back to the archery group." And she rushed off in the direction of the castle gateway.

Holly whirled round. The courtyard was packed with stalls and people. It wasn't going to be easy to find the Pooper – but the number of people milling around meant that Holly could search for him without Dad noticing.

"We'll have to check every stall," she told the Little Sparkles, "starting with this one." She pointed to a stall with a sign that said "Cuddly Castle Creatures" and began to rummage through the toy bats, rats, ravens and spiders on the table. The Little Sparkles jumped into a basket under the counter. Holly could hear them tinkling as they searched through the cuddly toys inside it. But the Pooper wasn't there.

"I'm going to check out the ice cream stand," Holly told the Little Sparkles. She walked over to the stall, which was shaded by a pretty pink parasol. "What flavours do you have?" Holly asked the ice cream seller.

"Vanilla, strawberry and chocolate," the girl said, lifting up a lid and showing her the big tubs of ice cream.

Holly peered in. The vanilla ice cream looked a bit strange. There was a muddy, wrinkly blob in the middle of it. The blob wriggled. It was the Pooper!

Holly felt in her pocket and took out a handful of change. "Please may I have a big scoop of vanilla from the middle of

the tub?" she asked, hoping the girl
would spoon up the Pooper. "That bit
looks – er – yummiest."

The girl peered at the tub of vanilla
and screwed up her face.

"Yuck!" she exclaimed. "It's full of dirt! I can't sell that!" And before Holly could stop her, the girl tipped the box of Pooper ice cream into the bin.

"The ice cream stand is closed until further notice," the girl announced to the queue of people. "Sorry!"

Everyone sighed and moved away. The Little Sparkles fluttered over to Holly.

"That naughty Pooper is spoiling their day!" Tubbs groaned.

Holly peered into the bin.

"Ugh!" she gasped.

The Pooper was sitting on a heap of smelly rubbish. Holly could make out melted ice cream, soggy cones, mouldy

apple cores and half-eaten hot dogs covered in mustard and tomato ketchup.

"Come on out, you silly old Pooper," she told him.

THHHPPP! The Pooper blew a raspberry in retort.

The Little Sparkles came up and looked over her shoulder.

"It's much nicer out here!" they called.

The Pooper chanted:

"Nicey-nice is what I hate!
I think this smelly bin is great!"

"I'll fish him out," Holly told the Little Sparkles. She carefully took off her pointy hat, held her breath, leaned into the disgusting bin and caught him. The Pooper was so covered in ice cream that he felt like a fistful of slippery slime.

BLUP! With a slurpy squelch, the Pooper wriggled free. He grabbed a corner of the bin bag and dashed off,

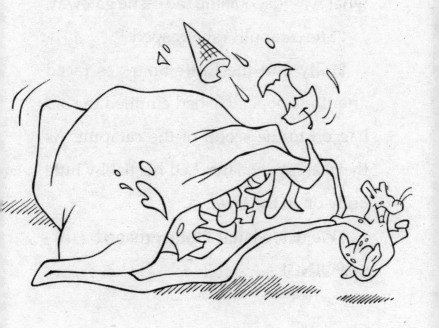

dragging the bag full of stinky rubbish behind him. He disappeared in the shadows of the gateway.

"Where's he going with that?" Holly wondered. She hurried to wash the goo off her fingers in a horse trough and put her hat back on. Then she remembered what was just outside the castle gateway.

"The catapult!" she gasped.

Holly and the Little Sparkles raced after the Pooper. He had emptied the bin bag on to the scoop of the catapult. As they ran up, he launched his flabby little body on to the lever.

"We're too late!" Holly groaned.

BOING!

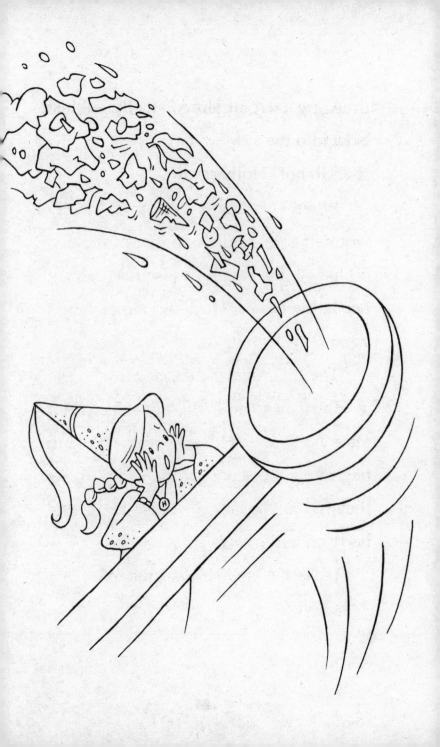

A great arc of slimy, smelly rubbish shot into the air.

"Oh no!" Holly cried.

6

Catapult Chaos

Over at the archery area, everyone was taking turns to fire arrows at the targets – except Rose. She was standing away from the group, wondering how Holly and the Little Sparkles were getting on.

A flash of movement caught her eye. A disgusting shower of rubbish was flying towards her. It had to be the Pooper up to his mischief!

She put her hands over her head to

protect herself from the slimy banana skins, chocolate wrappers, soggy chips and drippy ice cream. But before it could rain down on her, the arc of rubbish transformed into a beautiful glittering rainbow.

Rose gasped in amazement as the end of the rainbow touched down on the bouncy castle. She glanced at her friends and at Mum, but no one else had noticed it. The rainbow colours spread over the bouncy castle and it began to re-inflate, like magic. In the distance, she could just hear the tooting of tiny party blowers. It *was* magic – Little Sparkles magic!

Maybe they've already turned the Pooper into a new Little Sparkle, Rose thought. *I've got to find out!*

She told Mum that she was going to see what Holly was doing and hurried off, following the direction of the twinkling glitter trail in the sky.

The trail stopped at the catapult. The Little Sparkles were circling around it while Holly stood with her hands on her hips in front of the Pooper.

"You're surrounded," Holly was telling him. "You may as well give up."

"No. You'll try to turn me into a silly Little Sparkle!" The Pooper blobbed up the crossbar towards the catapult's scoop.

It rested on the ground like the heavy end of a seesaw.

"Can't catch me if I catapult," the Pooper said, and leapt on to the catapult lever.

"Don't, it's dangerous!" Rose cried.

But the scoop shot up. The Little Sparkles jangled in alarm as the Pooper threw himself into its path. The scoop swung up and rocketed the Pooper into the air.

"WHEEE!" the Pooper yelled.

Holly and Rose shaded their eyes and gazed upwards. As they watched, the Pooper's look of glee turned to fear as he realized how high up he was. His face screwed up in panic.

"Heeeeeeeelp! I'll be splatted!" he shrieked, waving his stubby arms about.

Holly and Rose looked from left to right, trying to think of a way to save him.

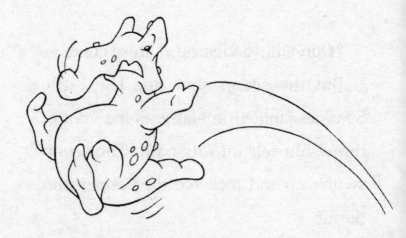

"The bouncy castle!" Rose exclaimed. "It's mended. It'll make a soft landing."

"Only if he comes down on it," Holly said.

"We'll make sure he does," barked Peppy. Like a flash of lightning, the Little Sparkles zipped towards the bouncy castle as the Pooper whizzed further through the air.

Holly looked over at Rose as they dashed after them.

Would they make it in time?

7

Bouncing Back

The Pooper was plummeting to the ground with his eyes tight shut. He was going to miss the soft landing of the bouncy castle by a whisker.

"He'll go splat!" Holly groaned. But just when it looked hopeless, there was a blaze of light. Tubbs, Peppy, Bubbles, Princess and Tikki had surrounded the bouncy castle with their magical glitter and it was shifting quickly towards the

Pooper's landing spot.

There was a rubbery BOING and the Pooper landed safely in the middle of the inflatable.

He opened his eyes. "Oh!" he cried out.

"Are you OK?" the girls shouted.

The Pooper turned to Holly and Rose and his surprise turned to panic. He tried to jump out over the top, but he was too small and squidgy to do it. He thumped down on his bottom.

"Stupid bouncy castle," he grumbled crossly.

"It's not stupid," Rose said. "It's fun!"

"That's it!" Holly whispered to Rose and the Little Sparkles. "If we can make him bounce up high, he'll have fun. Then he'll turn into a Little Sparkle!"

The Little Sparkles' tinkling laughter filled the air as Holly jumped on to the bouncy castle. She leaned down to hold the Pooper's sticky little hand.

"It's fun to bounce with friends," she told him.

"Get off me," the Pooper yelled, pulling his hand away. "Poopers aren't friends with princesses!"

This gave Rose an idea.

"Look, everyone! The bouncy castle is fixed!" she called across to the archery group. "Princess Holly and Princess Rose command you all to come and have a go!" Then she ran to tell the group who were making shields.

Mum, Dad and the party guests dropped what they were doing and raced to the inflatable castle. Within a minute, everyone was jumping up and down, having a great time.

BOING, BOING, BOING! People were springing about all over the place. The Pooper couldn't have stood still if he'd wanted to! He was going higher and higher into the air with every rebound. Rose nudged Holly.

"It's working!" she giggled as the Pooper's face became less and less frowny and more and more smiley. Soon he was chuckling in delight.

"This ... is ... FUN!" he yelled as rocketed into the air.

At the top of his jump, there was an explosion of glitter, like a tiny firework going off.

A little pink and green dragon flapped its sparkly wings and drifted down to land on the grassy meadow.

The Pooper had become a Little Sparkle!

8

A Very Happy Birthday

Rose and Holly clambered down from the bouncy castle. They and the Little Sparkles gathered around the tiny dragon that used to be a Pooper. Peppy took a silver balloon from his party bag and gave it to the new Little Sparkle, who wagged his twinkly tail.

"Look at my lovely new balloon," he said as it magically inflated.

Together, all the Little Sparkles sang:

*"Spread the lovely party joy to every
little girl and boy.
No more a grumpy Party
Pooper, make the parties
super duper."*

The twins waved as
the sparkling dragon
floated up and away.

"Now we need to fix the food and the games," Rose declared.

The Little Sparkles whispered to one another in their tinkling voices. They nodded their heads in agreement, then smiled at Holly and Rose. Tikki the kitten sang sweetly:

"Here's our birthday gift to you,
Sparkle magic for YOU to do!"

One by one, each Little Sparkle poured a tiny handful of shimmering hundreds-and-thousands into the twins' hands.

Holly and Rose felt their palms tingle.

They were holding on to magic!

"It's the best birthday present ever!"
Holly breathed.

"Quick!" Rose said. "While everyone's
still busy bouncing..."

The twins raced to the banqueting table. "One, two, three!" they counted together, then threw their hands into the air. A rainbow shower of hundreds-and-thousands sprinkled over the ruined food and broken games. The magic landed like a zillion tiny starbursts – and in an instant everything was as good as new!

Up until now, only the Little Sparkles had fixed the mess caused by the Poopers. Rose and Holly looked at each other in amazement.

"We did magic!" they gasped, and they jumped up and down and twirled around in joy.

"And we did it just in time," Holly

whispered, pointing. Mum, Dad and the party guests were coming towards them.

Holly and Rose blew each of the Little Sparkles a secret thank-you kiss.

"Wow!" Mum exclaimed. "Someone's fixed your party!'

"Whoever did this is really kind!" smiled Dad.

Mum nodded. "It's time to celebrate!"

She lit the candles on the cake and

everyone began to sing. The Little Sparkles jingled for joy as the twins blew out the candles and made a secret wish.

High above, and invisible to all the party guests, five tiny balloons appeared in the sky.

Rose and Holly looked up in wonder. Beneath each of the balloons was a tiny glittering creature: a dragon, a chick, a guinea pig, a seahorse and a parrot, each holding a party bag. They recognized them all – the five new Little Sparkles who used to be Poopers! The cheerful little creatures sang:

"Have fun on your special day
Hip-hip, hip-hip, hip-hip,
HOORAY!!!"

"My wish came true!" Holly said, holding out her hand to Rose. "I wanted to see the new Little Sparkles again!"

Rose took Holly's hand as she looked around at the beaming faces of their family and friends. The Little Sparkles twinkled among them, invisible to everyone except the twins.

"My wish came true, too," she breathed. "The Poopers have gone and now there are ten Little Sparkles to make parties fun for everyone!"

"We couldn't have done it without you!" Peppy woofed.

There was a rainbow flash of glitter as Princess, Bubbles, Tikki, Tubbs and the five new Little Sparkles nodded in agreement.

Holly and Rose shared a happy smile.

Thanks to their magical little friends,
their party was perfect!

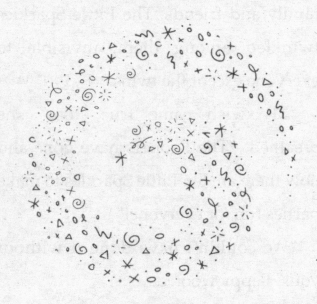

Don't miss the other

books in the series!